EYEWITNESS CLASSICS

DRACULA

A DK PUBLISHING BOOK

ABRIDGED FOR YOUNG READERS

Senior Editor Marie Greenwood
Series Art Editor Jane Thomas
Research Fergus Day
Production Katy Holmes
Managing Art Editor Chris Fraser
Picture Research Louise Thomas and Elizabeth Bacon
Abridgment Jo Fletcher-Watson
DTP Designer Kim Browne

To Mary, Theo, Dylan, and Max, with love – TH

First American Edition, 1997
2 4 6 8 10 9 7 5 3 1

Published in the United States by DK Publishing, Inc.
95 Madison Avenue, New York, New York 10016
Visit us on the World Wide Web at http://www.dk.com

Published in Great Britain by Dorling Kindersley Ltd.
A catalog record for this book is available from the Library of Congress.

ISBN0-7894-1489-9

Color reproduction by Bright Arts in Hong Kong
Printed by Graphicom in Italy

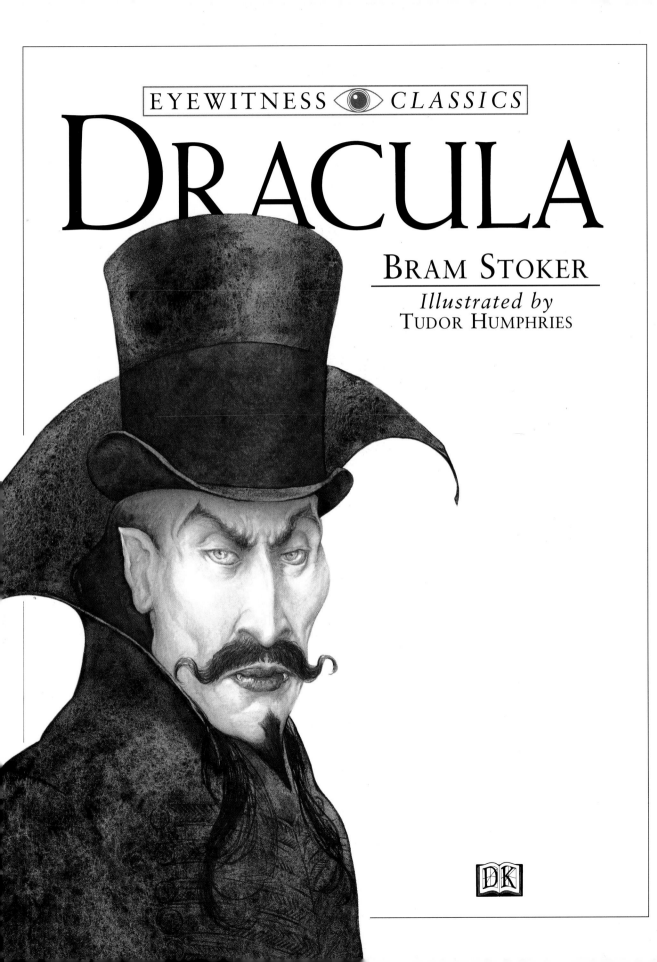

EYEWITNESS CLASSICS

DRACULA

BRAM STOKER

Illustrated by
TUDOR HUMPHRIES

DK

CONTENTS

Jonathan Harker

*Mina Murray,
Jonathan's fiancée*

Count Dracula

*Lucy Westenra,
Mina's friend*

Arthur Holmwood

Dr. John Seward

Professor Van Helsing

Quincey Morris

INTRODUCTION

Dracula may be the world's most famous vampire, but he was certainly not the first. Bloodsucking monsters have featured in folktales and myths in many parts of the world for a very long time. In the nineteenth century they began to appear in written form, and finally Bram Stoker's novel *Dracula* was published in 1897.

Stoker created the aristocratic character of Count Dracula and gave him a history connected with the real fifteenth-century Vlad Dracula. He introduced the possibility that the story had real roots in Transylvania. His settings for the story have inspired people to seek out Dracula's "original" castle in Romania as well as other landmarks that can be connected in some way to the story. Even though *Dracula* is a fictional work, people seem to want to find a true story behind the fantasy.

This *Eyewitness Classic* edition explores this fascinating background, placing Dracula firmly in his original context, where Bram Stoker created him.

Stoker's own words bring the famous character into focus. It was he who gave the world's favorite vampire his pointed ears, hairy palms, and long, sharp fingernails as well as long, sharp teeth. It was he who created the drama and tension, and the fear that pervades every scene of the tale.

The graveyard at Whitby, one of the settings in Dracula.

Dracula's Homeland

Transylvania

Today Transylvania is a province of Romania. In 1897, the region was part of Austro-Hungary.

The story starts when Jonathan Harker travels to Transylvania to do business with Count Dracula, who wants to buy a house in England. The word "Transylvania" means "The land beyond the forest." For Jonathan Harker it was a journey to the very edge of the world he knew.

Vlad Dracula

Bram Stoker gave his character Dracula a real ancestor – Vlad Dracula (c.1431-76), prince of Wallachia, an ancient kingdom now part of Romania.

Son of Dracul

Vlad's father was Vlad Dracul, meaning "devil" or "dragon." His son became known as Dracula, or "son of dracul."

Vlad Dracul was a knight of the Order of the Dragon.

The Order's emblem

Sighisoara

Vlad Dracula was born and brought up in Sighisoara, a medieval town in Transylvania.

House where Vlad was born

The Impaler

Vlad was a cruel tyrant who ordered thousands of people to be impaled on stakes, which earned him the name Vlad Tepes, or "Vlad the Impaler."

The landscape

Jonathan Harker saw a land of unspoiled beauty dotted with towns and villages.

Traditional Transylvanian craftware

Traditional peasant costume of Transylvania

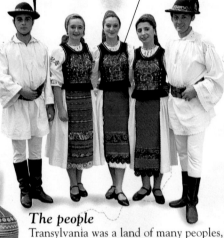

The people

Transylvania was a land of many peoples, including Magyars (from Hungary), Romanians, Szekelys, Slovaks, and gypsies. Out of this rich cultural mix grew a range of superstitions about vampires.

Gypsy culture

When gypsies settled in eastern Europe in the 1400s, they brought their vampire beliefs with them. The gypsies' name for vampire is *mullo*.

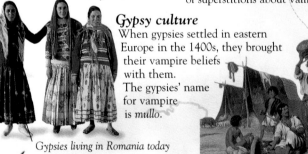

Gypsies living in Romania today

A gypsy camp from the 1900s

Vampire beliefs

The countries of eastern Europe share a history of vampire beliefs. Romanians, in particular, have many different names for vampires, such as a *strigoi*, a vampire who flies at night and sucks the blood of sleeping children.

Klausenburgh

Jonathan Harker traveled here by train from Budapest in Austro-Hungary. Klausenburgh was the great capital of Transylvania, and its many fine buildings are Hungarian in style. Today it is known by the Romanian name of Cluj.

Bistritz

It was in Bistritz, today called Bistrita, that Harker was first warned about the dangers of vampires. This hotel in Bistrita is called the *Coroana de aur* ("Golden Krone") after the inn where Harker stayed.

Borgo Pass

The Borgo Pass is one of the most dramatic settings in the novel. Set high up in the Carpathian Mountains, the Pass and the surrounding area are breathtaking, with sheer mountain faces and forests of fir trees.

VERESTI

Sereth River

Bistritza River

BISTRITZ

KLAUSENBURG

SIGHISOARA

HUNADOARA

Bran Castle

CARPATHIAN MOUNTAINS

CURTEA DE ARGES

DRACULA'S CASTLE

Dracula's home may have been based on a real castle in Romania. Various sites have been suggested:

1. Bran Castle, built in the 13th century, where Vlad the Impaler was both a guest and later a prisoner. Its dark rooms and corridors tie in with Bram Stoker's description.

2. The 13th-century castle at Hunadoara, where Vlad Dracul is believed to have been a guest.

3. The castle north of Curtea de Arges that Vlad the Impaler built and lived in.

Bran Castle

Wooden graveyard crosses from Transylvania

Old country borders

- - - - - New country borders

BUCHAREST

Night visits

Romanians believed that vampires tried to return home at night. They could be prevented by smearing garlic around the doors and windows.

At the graveside

A vampire's grave could be detected by the presence of holes around the graveside through which the vampire could appear, in the form of a mist. To prevent this, water was poured into the holes.

VARNA

The journey
On leaving Germany, Jonathan traveled through Europe before reaching Transylvania. He stopped at Klausenburgh, today called Cluj, the capital of Transylvania.

EASTERN EUROPE IN 1897

Germany

Austro-Hungary

Romania

We saw little towns or castles on the tops of steep hills.

Chapter one

JONATHAN HARKER'S DIARY

May 4

LEFT MUNICH ON MAY 1ST. The train reached Vienna early next morning, and later passed Budapest, which seems a wonderful place from the glimpse I got from the train window. After nightfall we came to Klausenburgh in Transylvania, and here I stopped for the night.

Before leaving London, I did some research on Transylvania. I thought it best that I knew something about the area before doing business with a nobleman of that country. I was not able to find Castle Dracula on any map, but I found that Bistritz, the town named in Count Dracula's letter, is a fairly well-known place. I did not sleep well that night, though my bed was comfortable enough. I had all sorts of strange dreams, and there was a dog howling all night under my window.

The train started early next morning and all day long we saw little towns or castles on the tops of steep hills.

It was twilight when we got to Bistritz. I went straight to the Golden Krone Hotel, as Count Dracula had directed. I was evidently expected for an elderly woman in peasant dress greeted me and gave me a letter:

My Friend,
Welcome to the Carpathians. I am anxiously expecting you. At three tomorrow take the stage coach for Bukovina. My carriage will await you at the Borgo Pass. I trust you will enjoy your stay in my beautiful land.
Your friend, Dracula

St. George's Day

In eastern Europe this feast day fell on May 5, after a night of fear. Today it is celebrated in many parts of Europe on April 23. St. George was believed to offer protection against vampires.

Sacred beads

Roman Catholics use a rosary – a sacred string of beads with a crucifix attached to it – for keeping count of a series of prayers.

When I asked my landlady if she knew Count Dracula, she made the sign of the cross and refused to speak further. But just before I left, she came up to my room and said in a very hysterical way:

"Must you go? Oh! Young Sir, must you go? Do you not know that it is the eve of St. George's Day, and tonight, when the clock strikes midnight, all the evil things in the world will have full sway?"

I told her that I was engaged on business, and must go. She took off her rosary and put it round my neck, and then left the room.

I am writing up this part of the diary while I wait for the coach. The rosary is still round my neck.
Whether it is my landlady's fear, or the many ghostly traditions of this place, or the crucifix itself, I do not know, but I am not feeling nearly as easy in my mind as usual. If this book should ever reach Mina before I do, let it bring my good-bye. Here comes the coach!

She put the rosary round my neck.

A carriage with four horses drove up behind us.

The Carpathians
The high, jagged Carpathian Mountains dominate the landscape of Transylvania. Bram Stoker had read about the Carpathians – a wild land of superstition and magic.

Roadside crosses
In Catholic countries like Transylvania, stone crosses were placed along the road for travelers to stop and pray.

When I climbed into the coach, I saw the driver talking with the landlady. I could hear certain words being repeated, such as *Ordog* – "Satan," and *vrolok* – "werewolf" or " vampire." Then the driver cracked his whip and we set off.

The road was rugged, but we seemed to fly over it with a feverish haste. Beyond green, swelling hills rose mighty slopes of forest up to the lofty Carpathians. As we wound on our endless way, and the sun sank lower and lower, the shadows of the evening began to creep round us. By the roadside there were many crosses, and as we swept by, my companions crossed themselves.

When it grew dark there seemed to be some excitement among the passengers, and they urged the driver to further speed. Then the mountains seemed to come nearer on each side and to frown down upon us as we entered the Borgo Pass. We flew along, the driver leaning forward, the passengers peering eagerly into the darkness. At last, we saw the Pass opening out on the eastern side. I looked out for the count's carriage, each moment expecting to see the glare of lamps through the blackness, but all was dark. I was already wondering what I had best do, when the horses began to neigh and snort and plunge wildly. Then, among a chorus of screams from the passengers, a carriage up beside our coach. The driver had a long beard and wore a great black hat, which seemed to hide his face. I could only see the gleam of a pair of very bright eyes, which seemed red in the lamplight.

"Give me the gentleman's luggage," said the strange driver. As he spoke he smiled, and the lamplight fell on a hard mouth with very red lips and sharp-looking teeth, as white as ivory. He helped me into his carriage with a hand that held my arm in a grip of steel. Without a word he shook the reins, the horses turned, and we swept into the darkness of the Pass.

By and by, I struck a match, and by its flame looked at my watch. It was close to midnight. I waited with a sick feeling of suspense.

Then, from the mountains on each side of us there began a loud and sharp howling – that of wolves. The driver swept his arms, and the wolves fell back and disappeared. We kept on ascending, now in almost complete darkness, for the rolling clouds obscured the moon. Eventually, I fell into a fearful sleep.

Werewolf
According to legend, a werewolf was a man or woman who changed into a wolf and attacked people and other animals.

Wolves
Wolves hunt in packs and howl to each other to signal where they are. In some cultures, the wolf is a bad omen.

"Give me the gentleman's luggage," said the strange driver.

I suddenly woke to find the driver pulling up in the courtyard of a vast, ruined castle from whose tall black windows came no ray of light, and whose broken battlements showed a jagged line against

BRAN CASTLE
Bram Stoker may have modeled his description of Dracula's castle on Bran Castle in Romania.

The broken battlements showed a jagged line against the moonlit sky.

Hidden yard
Bran Castle has an inner courtyard with secret underground passageways and escape routes.

the moonlit sky. He helped me to alight, then carriage and all disappeared down one of the dark openings. After what seemed an endless time, I heard a heavy step behind the great door, and saw through the chinks the gleam of a coming light. There was the sound of rattling chains and the clanking of massive bolts being drawn back. A key was turned, and the door swung open.

Within stood a tall old man with a long white mustache, clad in black from head to foot. He held in his hand an antique silver lamp, the flame throwing quivering shadows as it flickered. He motioned me in, saying: "Welcome to my house. Enter freely and of your own will." He did not step toward me, but stood like a statue, as though his gesture of welcome had turned him to stone. But as soon as I stepped inside, he grasped my hand with a hand as cold as ice – more like the hand of a dead than a living man.

"Count Dracula?" I asked.

"I am Dracula; and I bid you welcome, Mr. Harker, to my house."

He led me to a well-lit room where a table was set for supper. My host stood, leaning against a mighty fireplace in which the logs flamed and flared. He made a graceful wave of his hand to the table, and said: "I pray you, be seated. You will, I trust, excuse me that I do not join you, but I have dined already."

When I finished eating, I observed him. His face was strong, with peculiarly arched nostrils. The mouth under the heavy mustache was fixed and cruel-looking with sharp white teeth over the lips, which were remarkably red for a man his age. His ears were pale and pointed. His nails were long and fine, and cut to a sharp point. Strange to say, there were hairs in the centers of his palms.

As he leaned toward me, a horrible feeling of sickness came over me, and the count, noticing, drew back. I looked toward the window to see the first streaks of dawn, and heard the howling of many wolves. The count's eyes gleamed. "Listen to them – the children of the night. What music they make." Then he rose, saying, "You must be tired. Your bedroom is ready. I will be away until tomorrow, so sleep well."

He held in his hand an antique silver lamp, the flame throwing quivering shadows as it flickered.

 *May 8*

There is something so strange about this place and all that is in it that I cannot help feeling uneasy. I wish I was safely out of it, or that I had never come. I stayed up all night with the count and we talked over the legal requirements of buying Carfax, the house east of London that my firm has found for him.

I slept only a few hours, but it was dark in the afternoon when I got up. I hung my shaving glass by my window, and began to shave. Suddenly, I felt a hand on my shoulder, and heard the count's voice saying, "Good morning." I started, cutting myself slightly. I greeted the count and turned to shave once more. To my amazement, there was no reflection of the count in the mirror, though he was standing behind my shoulder. I saw that the cut had bled a little and the blood was trickling over my chin. I looked round for some plaster. When the count saw my face, his eyes blazed and he suddenly grabbed at my throat. Then his hand touched the string of beads that held the crucifix and his fury passed so quickly that I could hardly believe it had been there.

Marking the map
Count Dracula has a map of the British Isles on which three places are circled: London, Exeter (Jonathan's home), and Whitby.

Leather pouch for holding razors

Razor sharp
To ensure a sharp blade for every shave, travelers took one razor for every day of the week.

Brush

Cut-throat razor

Ivory handle

Ebony handle

"Take care how you cut yourself," he said. "It is more dangerous than you think in this country."

He opened the heavy window with one wrench of his

terrible hand and flung out the mirror, which shattered into a thousand pieces on the stone courtyard far below. Then he withdrew without a word.

When I went into the dining room, breakfast was prepared, but I could not find the count anywhere. So I ate alone. It is strange that as yet I have not seen the count eat or drink. He must be a very peculiar man!

After breakfast I explored the castle and found a room facing south. The castle is on the edge of a cliff. A stone falling from the window could fall a thousand feet without touching anything. When I had seen the view I explored further and further; doors, doors, doors everywhere, all locked and bolted. In no place except the windows in the walls is there an exit. I begin to be afraid that the castle is a prison, and that I am a prisoner.

No reflection

Mirrors were used in the ceremonies of many ancient religions. Followers believed that mirrors reflect the soul, and that evil beings had no soul to reflect.

Ancient Egyptian mirror

When the count saw my face, his eyes blazed and he grabbed at my throat.

VLAD DRACULA
One of Dracula's "noble ancestors" was the terrifying Vlad Dracula. Vlad tortured and killed up to 40,000 victims. It was said that his crimes had no equal, even among the most bloodthirsty of tyrants. Vlad's family emblem, used on his coins, was the dragon. He tested the loyalty of his subjects by disguising himself and leaving coins in shops and public places; anyone pocketing them was executed.

Vlad's coins

Cruel tyrant
It was said that after defeating his enemies in 1460, Vlad enjoyed a meal among the impaled bodies of his victims.

When I realized I was imprisoned, I rushed up and down like a rat in a trap. Then the great castle door closed with a thud and I knew the count had returned. I crept to my room and, through the crack in the door, saw him make my bed. He had no servants! It was he who had driven the carriage. It was he who controlled the wolves with a wave of his hand – a terrible thought. Why did the people at Bistritz and on the coach fear for me? I blessed the good woman who hung the crucifix round my neck, for it comforts me when I touch it. I must find out all I can about Count Dracula.

May 12.

We talked this evening about Transylvanian history, and the count described the brave deeds of all his noble ancestors.

He retired to do some work, and I went back to the room with the view south. From the corner of my eye I saw something move a story below me. It was the count's head coming out of a window. I watched in terror as the whole man slowly emerged and began to crawl down the castle wall, face down, with his cloak spreading around him like great wings. At first I could not believe my eyes. I thought it was some trick of the moonlight, some weird effect of shadow, but I saw the fingers and toes grasp the stones. By using every corner the count moved downward with great speed, as a lizard moves along a wall. What kind of man or creature is this? I feel the dread of this horrible place and am surrounded by terrors I dare not think of . . .

His cloak spread around him like great wings.

FEMALE VAMPIRES

Female vampires appear in tales and legends from all over the world.

Lamia

This female vampire appears in many ancient legends. She was believed to be very beautiful and highly dangerous, especially to men and children.

Lilith

This vampire, also known as the Queen of the Night, appears in ancient Babylonian and Hebrew legends. According to one version, she was created to be Adam's wife, but left to join the evil forces of darkness.

Striges

This bird-vampire was a type of witch that could change into a bird at night and drink human blood.

May 15

Once again I watched the count crawl from his window. When I was sure he had left the castle I took the opportunity to explore more than I had dared to yet. Eventually, I found a door at the top of a stairway which opened a little way when I pushed hard against it. Inside, the windows were curtainless and the furniture was dusty with age. It was evening and I felt suddenly sleepy, so I pulled up a great couch and lay down, not caring about the dust.

I suppose I must have fallen asleep, but my dream was startlingly real. In the moonlight opposite me were three young women. They came close to me and looked at me for some time, and then whispered together. Two had dark hair and had great piercing eyes that seemed to be almost red when contrasted with the pale yellow moon. The other was fair, with great, wavy masses of golden hair and eyes like pale sapphires. All three had brilliant white teeth that shone like pearls against their ruby lips. There was something about them that made me uneasy, some longing and at the same time some deadly fear. Then the fair-haired girl bent over me till I could feel her hot breath on my neck. Lower and lower went her head as the lips went below my mouth and chin and seemed about to fasten on my throat. My skin began to tingle and I could just feel the hard dents of two sharp teeth. I closed my eyes and waited with beating heart.

In the moonlight opposite me were three young women.

But at that instant the count appeared. As my eyes opened involuntarily, I saw his strong hand grasp the woman's slender neck and hurl her from me. His face was deathly pale and he spoke in a furious whisper: "How dare you touch him, any of you? This man belongs to me!" At this, the women let out a low ripple of hard, soulless laughter and simply seemed to fade into the rays of the moonlight.

Loogaroo
This witch-vampire appears in West Indian legends. The name comes from the French loup garou, *meaning "shape-changer."*

May 28

There is a chance of escape! A band of gypsies have arrived at the castle and camped in the courtyard. I have read that there are thousands of gypsies in Transylvania.

I have written a letter in shorthand to Mina, explaining my situation, and thrown it, with a gold piece, through the bars of my window. I made signs that I wanted it posted. A man took the letter, pressed it to his heart, then put it in his cap. I can do no more.

The count has come. He sat down beside me and began to open an envelope. As he caught sight of the strange symbols inside, a dark look came into his face, and his eyes blazed wickedly. "This letter is not signed, so it cannot matter to us." He calmly held letter and envelope in the flame of the lamp till they were consumed. Then he left the room.

Later, as I was sitting on my bed trying to think of a plan, I heard the cracking of whips and the scraping of horses' feet. With joy I hurried to the window and saw drive into the yard two great wagons, brought by Slovaks. They were wearing wide

Shorthand
The shorthand that Jonathan used may have been Pitman's. First issued in 1837, it was widely used by the 1890s.

Gypsies
Originally from northern India, many gypsies settled in Transylvania in the 1400s. They were divided into groups according to occupation, such as the lingurari (spoon-makers) above.
Today, gypsies make up about 10 percent of the Romanian population.

hats, great nail-studded belts, sheepskin, and high boots. I ran to the door, intending to join them and escape, but – again, a shock – I had been locked in. I rushed back to the window and cried to them for help. They looked up, then pointed at me and laughed. After that, no effort of mine would make them even look at me.

Helplessly, I watched them unload the wagons, which contained great boxes. These must have been empty because they carried them easily. When all the

Slovaks
Stoker had never actually seen Slovak people, but knew they lived in Transylvania at the time.

Slovaks wore sheepskin coats and wide belts – the typical dress of the Romanian peasant.

boxes had been piled in one corner of the courtyard, the Slovaks were given some money by the gypsies. Shortly afterward, I heard the cracking of whips and the Slovaks drove their wagons out of the castle courtyard.

I hurried to the window and saw drive into the yard two great wagons.

DRACULA'S HOME
In Bran Castle, heavy oak doors lead into gloomy rooms that house ornate furniture.

Four-poster bed carved in wood

Wrought-iron candlestick

June 25

There, in one of the boxes, on a pile of earth, lay the count!

I have not yet seen the count in daylight. Can it be that he sleeps when others are awake and is awake while they sleep? His bedroom door is always locked, so the only way I can find out is to climb in through his window!

While I still had the courage, I ventured out of my window and climbed down the great stones of the castle wall till I reached the count's windowsill. I slid in through the window feet first and, to my surprise, I found the room was empty. In one corner was a heavy door. It opened when I tried it, and led to a circular stairway. I descended and found myself in an old, ruined chapel. There was a sickly smell of newly turned earth, and I saw that the ground had recently been dug up and the earth placed in great wooden boxes – the same ones that the gypsies had brought. I went over to examine them, counting fifty in all, and then I saw something which filled my soul with horror. There, in one of the boxes, on a pile of earth, lay the count! But he looked like a young man, for his

white hair had
turned iron-gray
and his lips were red with blood.
There was a mocking smile on his
bloated face which seemed to drive me mad. I seized a shovel and
lifted it to strike the monster. But as I did so the head turned, and
the blazing eyes looked at me. I was paralyzed with fear, and the
shovel slipped, only making a gash above his forehead.

Suddenly, I heard the sound of footsteps. I ran back up to the
count's room and heard below me the grinding of a key in a lock.
Then I heard the boxes being hammered closed and carried away.

Now I am alone in the castle. I must try to climb down the wall
and find a way out of this dreadful place.

Winding stairs
*Circular staircases
were common in
castles. These
wooden stairs
are from Bran
Castle, and
lead up to a
secret back
entrance into
rooms on the
floor above.*

I came up here an hour ago with Lucy, and we had a most interesting talk.

WHITBY
The seaside town of Whitby lies at the mouth of the Esk River in Yorkshire, England. Bram Stoker spent several vacations here and knew the town well.

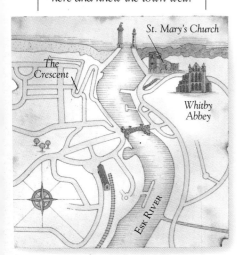

St. Mary's Church

The Crescent

Whitby Abbey

ESK RIVER

Chapter two

MINA MURRAY'S DIARY

July 24, Whitby

LUCY MET ME AT THE STATION, looking sweeter than ever, and we drove up to her mother's house at the Crescent. This is a lovely place. The little river, the Esk, runs through a deep, green valley, which broadens out at as it comes near the harbor. On either side of the harbor mouth, stone piers stretch out to sea with a lighthouse at the end of each one. Outside the harbor there is a reef, and at one end of it is a buoy with a bell that swings in bad weather.

The houses of the town are all red-roofed and look as if they

are piled on top of each other up the cliffside. Above the town is the ruin of Whitby Abbey. It is a most noble ruin, and is reached by a clifftop walk.

Between the abbey and the town is a parish church, surrounded by a large graveyard. This, I think, is the nicest spot in Whitby. It lies right over the town, and has a beautiful view of the harbor. There are paths through the churchyard, with seats beside them.

I came up here an hour ago with Lucy, and we had a most interesting talk. She told me all about her beloved Arthur and their coming marriage. It made me just a little heartsick, for I haven't heard from Jonathan for over a month. I wonder where he is and if he is thinking of me. I wish he were here.

Whitby Abbey
Each year, people climb 199 steps to see the impressive abbey ruins.

August 6

Still no news from Jonathan, but now I am anxious about Lucy, too. She has taken to her old habit of walking in her sleep, and has grown very pale. Lucy's mother is naturally worried about her, and has asked me to keep the door of our bedroom locked every night. There is a strange restlessness about Lucy which I do not understand; even in her sleep she seems to be watching me. She tries the door, and finding it locked, goes about the room searching for the key.

This evening Lucy is more excitable than ever. As I write there are thick clouds gathering, ready for a storm. The fishing boats are racing for home.

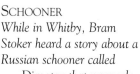

SCHOONER
While in Whitby, Bram Stoker heard a story about a Russian schooner called Dimetry *that narrowly missed a ridge of rocks in the harbor.*

CUTTING FROM THE DAILYGRAPH, AUGUST 8, WHITBY
(Pasted in Mina Murray's diary)

One of the greatest storms on record has just been experienced here. A little after midnight the tempest broke. White-crested waves rushed up the cliffs and crashed over the piers. On the East Cliff, the new searchlight picked out a schooner with all its sails set, traveling at great speed toward the harbor. As she got nearer the searchlight showed that, lashed to the helm, was a man's body. A great awe came over all of us on the shore as we realized the ship was unsteered save by the hand of a dead man! But the schooner did not slow – it

The ship was unsteered save by the hand of a dead man!

rushed across the harbor and pitched onto the sand and gravel by the East Cliff. Then, the very instant it touched the shore, an immense dog sprang up on deck from below and jumped onto the sand. It headed straight for the steep cliff and disappeared into the darkness.

August 9

It turns out that the schooner has come from Varna, and is called the *Demeter*. Her only cargo is a number of great wooden boxes filled with mold. I have been permitted to read the captain's logbook and have found out the details of the ship's voyage. At first the crew reported that there was something strange on board; then, one by one, the men disappeared until only the captain was left. Being an honorable sailor he refused to leave his ship but tied his hands to the wheel, and with them a crucifix, to save his soul from the fiend below deck.

No trace was ever found of the great dog.

Navigation
The captain plotted a journey before sailing, using maps and navigational instruments. A compass was used to measure bearings, or changes of direction.

Ship's compass

Logbook
The captain kept notes of the ship's progress in his logbook, along with any interesting events along the way.

Full moon
It was believed that a full moon made night creatures, like wolves and bats, more active. Some vampire stories say that it was the rays of the full moon that revived the vampire from his deathly sleep.

Night wanderings
Sleepwalking is a condition that occurs during the deepest sleep, and is most common in children. The sleeper walks around mechanically, usually with the eyes open. It was believed that if a person sleepwalked it could lead to a relative, often a brother, becoming a vampire.

August 11

Last night I woke up with a horrible sense of fear. Lucy was not in her bed, and the door was not locked, as I had left it. I did not want to wake her mother, who has been ill recently, so I threw on some clothes and ran downstairs. In the hall I saw, with a chill in my heart, that the front door was open. I took a big shawl and ran out. The clock was striking one as I was in the Crescent, and there was not a soul in sight.

At the edge of the West Cliff I looked across the harbor toward the abbey. There was a bright full moon, and on our favorite seat I saw a figure. My knees trembled as I climbed up the endless steps to the abbey. When I got near the top, I called in fright, "Lucy! Lucy!" Something long and black was bending over the half-reclining figure; it raised its head and I could see red, gleaming eyes. But when I reached the seat I found Lucy quite alone and still asleep. I flung the warm shawl around her for I dreaded she would get some deadly chill from the night air. I fastened the shawl at her throat with a big safety pin. But I must have been clumsy and pricked her, for she put her hand to her throat and moaned.

I shook her several times, till finally she awoke. She clung to me as we walked home, and when we got back to the house I tucked her into bed. I was sorry to notice how much my clumsiness with the safety pin had hurt her. The skin of her throat was pierced and on her nightdress was a drop of blood.

August 17

I have not had the heart to write in the last few days. Some sort of shadowy pall seems to be coming over our happiness. No news from Jonathan, and Lucy seems to be growing weaker. I do not understand Lucy's fading away as she is doing. She eats well and sleeps well, and enjoys the fresh air; but all the time the roses in her cheeks are fading, and she gets weaker day by day. At night she gets up and sits at the open window. The tiny wounds on her neck have not healed, if anything, they are larger than before.

My visit is coming to an end, and I must soon return
home, though I do worry about leaving Lucy. Arthur has
just visited and was much grieved on seeing her, she is so low in
spirits. He is writing to his friend, Dr. Seward.

*Something long and black
was bending over the half-
reclining figure.*

Chapter three

D<small>R.</small> S<small>EWARD'S</small> DIARY

September 4

I HAVE VISITED LUCY. She looks ill, although she does not seem to be suffering from any disease. I could easily see that she lacks blood but there are none of the usual anemic signs. She complained of difficulty in breathing and of heavy, lethargic sleep, with dreams that frighten her.

I understand now why Arthur is so anxious about her. I am in some doubt about her condition, though, so I have contacted my old friend and master, Professor Van Helsing, of Amsterdam. He is one of the most advanced scientists of his day, and knows as much about obscure diseases as anyone in the world.

September 12

Van Helsing has arrived. When I described Lucy's symptoms – the same as before, but infinitely more marked – he looked very grave, but said nothing.

We arrived at the house and Mrs. Westenra showed us into Lucy's room. I was horrified when I saw her. She was ghastly, chalkily pale; the red seemed to have gone even from her lips.

Lack of blood

Anemia is caused by a lack of iron in the blood. The sufferer becomes pale, weak, and very tired.

Her breathing was painful to hear. Van Helsing's face grew set as marble, and his eyebrows converged till they almost touched over his nose. Lucy lay motionless and did not seem to have strength to speak, so for a while we were all silent. Then Van Helsing beckoned to me, and we went gently out of the room.

We returned the next day and the professor brought with him a great bundle of white flowers.

"These are for you, Miss Lucy," he said.

"For me? Oh, Dr. Van Helsing!"

"Yes, my dear, but not for you to play with. These are medicines."

She smelled them, then said with a half-laugh, "Why, professor, I believe you are playing a joke on me! These flowers are only common garlic."

To my surprise, Van Helsing rose up and said sternly, "I never jest! There is a grim purpose in all I do. Take care, for the sake of others, if not for your own." Then seeing poor Lucy scared, he went on more gently: "Oh, my dear, do not fear me. I am only doing this for your own good. I will place them in your room and make a wreath out of them for you to wear. Come with me, friend John, and you shall help me deck the room with my garlic."

"Well, professor," I said, "I know you always have a reason for what you do, but this certainly puzzles me. It is as if you were working some spell to keep out an evil spirit."

"Perhaps I am," he answered quietly.

"Oh, my dear, do not fear me. I am only doing this for your own good."

Van Helsing – the classic vampire hunter – has been portrayed in movies by many well-known actors, including Sir Anthony Hopkins (above).

Medical expert
Van Helsing was an expert in medicine and science. This reflected the mood of the time, which saw great advances in these fields.

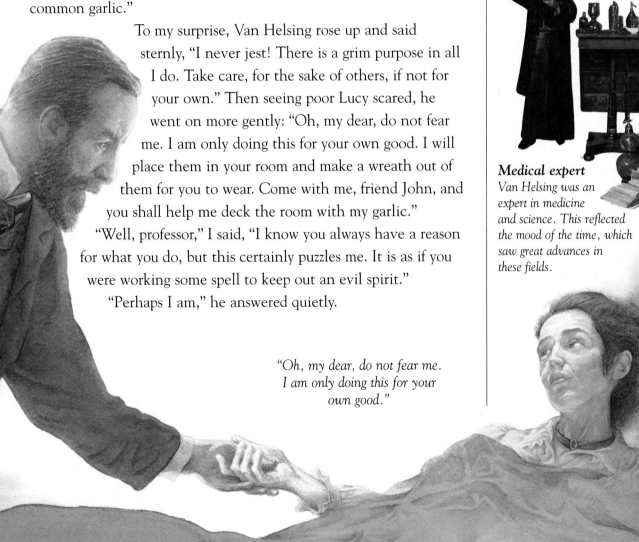

September 15

Van Helsing and I arrived at eight the next morning. Mrs. Westenra greeted us warmly. "You will be glad to know that Lucy is better. The dear child is still asleep. I looked into her

room and saw her, but did not go in, in case I disturbed her."

The professor smiled and said: "Aha! My treatment is working."

"You must not take all the credit, professor. Lucy's improved state is partly due to me."

"What do you mean ma'am?"

"Well, I was anxious about the dear child in the night, and went into her room. She was sleeping soundly, but the room was very stuffy. There were a lot of those horrible, strong-smelling flowers about everywhere, and she even had a bunch of them round her neck. I feared that the heavy odor would be too much for the dear child in her weak state, so I took them away and opened the window to let in some fresh air."

The professor turned ashen gray. Together we went up to Lucy's room. I drew up the blind and, as the morning sunshine flooded in, we saw her face was whiter than ever. "You must remain here tonight and do not take your eyes from her," Van Helsing told me. Then he left to consult his medical books.

I sat by Lucy's bedside all night and watched her sleep peacefully. In the morning she awoke with renewed strength. The professor did not return so I decided to keep watch for another night. Lucy saw that I was worn out.

"No sitting up for you tonight. I am quite well again," she said. I did not argue, and let her show me to a room next to her own where I would be able to hear if she called out. I lay on the sofa and fell asleep immediately. I was woken by the professor's hand on my head. The whole night had passed and the patient had been left alone. We hurried to Lucy's room, and with trembling hands we opened the door.

Together we went up to Lucy's room.

The fireplace
Victorian houses were heated by open fires. Van Helsing rubbed garlic around the fireplace in case Dracula turned himself into wisps of smoke and came down the chimney.

Garlic flower

Garlic
Since ancient times, garlic has been used as a healing plant. Its strong smell was believed to ward off evil spirits and vampires.

Garlic clove

How shall I describe what we saw? On the bed lay Lucy and her mother. Mrs. Westenra had a look of terror fixed on her face. Lucy's face was white and the flowers had been removed from her neck so her throat was bare, showing the two wounds. The professor bent over the bed, and discovered that neither of the women was breathing.

Memorandum left by Lucy Westenra

This is an exact record of what took place tonight. I have barely strength to write, but it must be done.

I went to bed as usual, taking care that the flowers were placed as Dr. Van Helsing directed, and soon fell asleep. I was woken by flapping at the window. Then outside in the shrubbery I heard a howl, like a dog's. I went to the window and looked out, but could see nothing, except a big bat, which must have been buffeting its wings against the window. I went back to

bed again. Presently the door opened and my mother looked in; seeing that I was not asleep she came and sat by me. After a while we heard the low howl again, and shortly after there was a crash at the window, and broken glass was hurled onto the floor. Through the broken pane came the head of a great gray wolf. Mother cried out in fright and clutched wildly at anything around her. She tore the wreath of flowers from my neck. Then she fell over, as if struck by lightning. I kept my eyes fixed on the window, but the wolf drew his head back and a cloud of little specks, like dust, came blowing in through the broken pane, and circled round me. I tried to move but there was some spell upon me, and I remembered no more for a while. When I regained consciousness I could hear the howl of the wolf outside. My dear mother gone! It is time that I go, too. Good-bye, dear Arthur. God keep you, and God help me!

Piccadilly
This busy street in London, England, runs from Hyde Park Corner to Piccadilly Circus.

Fangs
There is little mention of fangs in vampire folklore. Fanged vampires made their first appearance in the literature of the 19th century.

Jonathan clutched my arm so tight.

Chapter four

MINA HARKER'S DIARY

September 22

JONATHAN HAS RETURNED TO ME. He has been ill; that is why he did not write. He has had some terrible shock, and does not seem to remember anything that has happened to him. But now we are married and are in Exeter together.

Our wedding service, in London, was very simple and very solemn. Afterward we took a bus to Hyde Park Corner and walked down Piccadilly. I was looking at a beautiful girl, in a big hat, when suddenly I felt Jonathan clutch my arm so tight that he hurt me. He was gazing at a tall, thin man with a black mustache, who was also observing the pretty girl. His face was not a good face; it was hard and cruel and his big white teeth, that looked all the whiter because his lips were so red, were pointed like an animal's.

"It is the man himself! It is the count, but he has grown young." cried Jonathan.

I led him away quietly and he soon became calmer. But I am afraid this has made him ill again. I must somehow learn the facts of his journey abroad, though I'm afraid to ask him, for fear I do more harm than good. The time is come when I must open his diary and know what is written.

When we arrived home we found a telegram from Van Helsing. Poor Lucy has died. And her mother, too. What a wealth of sorrow in a few words! And poor Arthur, to have lost such sweetness out of his life. God help us all to bear our troubles.

September 24

I hadn't the heart to write last night; that terrible diary of Jonathan's upset me so. How he must have suffered, whether it be true or only imagination. Did he get brain fever, and then write all those terrible things; or had he some cause for it all? I suppose I shall never know, for I dare not open the subject to him . . .

Professor Van Helsing has been to visit. He must be a good man if he looked after Lucy so well. I told him all I knew about Lucy's illness, and took the opportunity to ask him about Jonathan. Then I gave him Jonathan's journal. After he had read it he told me that, strange and terrible as it is, he believes it is true! What evil there is in the world. And how awful to think that the count is in London! Van Helsing is the man to hunt him down and Jonathan will help him.

"It is the count, but he has grown young."

After some time we saw a
white figure advancing.

Chapter five

Dr. Seward's diary

September 26

Crucifix
*A crucifix is a sacred
Christian symbol. It is in
Dracula that the crucifix
was first used as a powerful
tool against vampires.*

A crucifix is a cross with
the figure of Christ on it.

TODAY VAN HELSING BOUNDED INTO MY ROOM and
thrust last night's *Westminster Gazette* into my hand.
"What do you think of that?" he asked, pointing out a
paragraph about children being attacked in Hampstead. I read

that the victims had small wounds on their throats. "It is like poor Lucy's," I said, and asked the professor what this meant. "We cannot understand all the mysteries of life and death. But I want you to believe in things that you cannot," said the Professor quietly.

He covered his face with his hands. "Those marks on the children's throats were made by Lucy!"

"Are you mad?" I asked angrily.

"I wish I was," he replied.

He took a key to her tomb from his pocket and said, "Tonight I go to prove it. Dare you come with me?"

I plucked up what courage I had and agreed to go.

It was dark when we reached the churchyard. We found the Westenra tomb and the professor unlocked the creaky door. He lit a candle and found Lucy's coffin. Then he lifted off the lid. It was empty. This shocked me but Van Helsing was not surprised.

"Do you believe me now, my friend?" he said. Then he put on the lid again and blew out the candle. We went out and waited in the churchyard. After some time we saw a white figure advancing. My own heart grew cold as ice as I recognized the features of Lucy Westenra, but yet how changed. Her lips were crimson with blood and when she saw us she drew back with an angry snarl, such as a cat gives when taken unawares; then her eyes ranged over us. Van Helsing sprang in front of her and held out his golden crucifix. She recoiled from it and dashed past him; then we both watched in horrified amazement as she passed through a narrow crack in the door of the tomb.

Highgate Cemetery
The churchyard was probably based on Highgate Cemetery, in north London.

When she saw us she drew back with an angry snarl.

Klaus Kinski in the title role of the 1979 movie *Nosferatu: the Vampyre*

Nosferatu
This word comes from the Greek for "plague-carrier," which is how vampires were often described. Later it came to mean "vampire" or "un-dead" in Romanian.

Arthur placed the point of the stake over Lucy's heart.

September 27

Van Helsing met with myself, Arthur, and an American friend of his called Quincey Morris. The professor described the events of the previous night and told us there was a serious duty to be done. Then he asked Arthur for permission to enter Lucy's tomb again, and open the coffin.

"Is this some monstrous joke?" Arthur asked angrily.

Van Helsing went on, with an effort: "Miss Lucy is not dead. But she is not alive. She was bitten by the vampire when she was sleep-walking. Now she is un-dead, or nosferatu. If she lives, more of these children will be in her power. But if she dies then the wounds in in their throats will disappear. It is our duty to lay her to rest – and the one who loved her should set her free. This must be done while she sleeps, in the daytime. All I ask is that you come with me."

"It is hard to think of it and I cannot understand, but I will do as you wish," said Arthur in a broken voice.

We got to the churchyard by half-past-one, and waited until we had the place to ourselves. Van Helsing unlocked the tomb and lit a lantern. When we lifted the coffin lid, we all looked and I heard Arthur gasp as he saw the body lying there. A foul Thing, with pointed teeth

Burial rites
The idea of vampires sleeping in coffins began in the 19th century, when coffins came into general use.

and bloodstained mouth, had taken Lucy's shape.

"Tell me what I am to do?" said Arthur hoarsely, and his face was as pale as snow.

"Take this stake in your left hand and the hammer in your right. Then strike in God's name," Van Helsing explained. Arthur placed the point of the stake over Lucy's heart, then struck with all his might. The Thing in the coffin writhed and the teeth champed together. Finally it lay still. The terrible task was over.

Vampire legends
Legends of vampirelike creatures appear all over the world. The Indian goddess Kali was said to drink her victims' blood, yet was a life-giver to her followers.

Power over things
Vampires are said to have the ability to change the weather, create storms, and control many animals, including the creatures of the night.

Moth

Owl

Fox

Chapter six

Mina Harker's diary

September 30

JONATHAN AND I JOINED PROFESSOR VAN HELSING, Arthur, and Mr. Morris at Dr. Seward's house. The professor sat at the head of the table and started our meeting.

"I think I should tell you something of the enemy with which we have to deal. There are such beings as vampires. These vampires do not die, but grow in strength. They are known to exist everywhere, in ancient Greece and Rome, in Germany, France, India, and China.

"The vampire which is among us is as strong as twenty men; more cunning than any mortal; he can appear in different forms, and he can direct the elements: the storm, the fog, the thunder. He can command the meaner things: the owl, the bat, the moth, the fox, and the wolf. We have seen that he can even grow younger. He can transform himself into a wolf, as we gather from the ship that arrived in Whitby. He can be a bat, as Lucy saw at her bedroom window. He can grow and become small. How, then, can we destroy him? It will be a terrible task but

"There are such beings as vampires."

I believe it is our duty. What do you think?"

We all agreed without hesitation, and took a solemn vow on it.

The bat flew away
into the wood.

Changing shape
The vampire can turn into many different animals, including wolves and bats.

This is the vampire bat of South America, so-called because it feeds off the blood of mammals.

Sunset
A vampire's powers were weakest between sunrise and sunset. Vampires attacked at night, a time long associated with evil happenings.

"Let us consider the limitations of the vampire. His power ceases at the coming of day, and he can only change his form at exact sunrise and sunset. When we find this man-that-was, we can destroy him."

While the professor was talking, Mr. Morris was looking steadily at the window, and he now got up quietly and went out of the room. There was a pause, then the professor continued:

"Jonathan has found papers relating to the purchase of the count's house, Carfax. He has also discovered that the earth boxes were transported from Whitby to Carfax. We must find these boxes –"

There suddenly came the sound of a pistol shot. A window was shattered by a bullet, which struck the far wall of the room. Arthur rushed over to the window and threw open the sash. We heard Quincey Morris's voice outside:

"Sorry I frightened you. But while the professor was talking, a big

bat came and sat on the windowsill. I went out to have a shot, but it flew away into the wood."

Mr. Morris rejoined our group and Van Helsing went on:

"We must sterilize the earth so that he can no longer seek safety in the boxes. I say we have a look in his house right now. Mina, you must stay here, you are too precious to risk."

All the men seemed relieved at this suggestion; but it did not seem right that I should be left out of their plan. Now they have gone to Carfax.

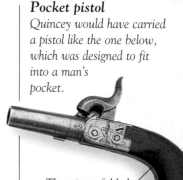

Pocket pistol
Quincey would have carried a pistol like the one below, which was designed to fit into a man's pocket.

The trigger folded into the pistol when not in use.

We took care to keep in the shadows of the trees.

Crossroads

"Carfax" is from an old French word meaning "crossroads." Suicides were often buried at crossroads, and they, it was believed, could become vampires.

Chapter seven

Jonathan Harker's diary

October 1

WE ARRIVED AT CARFAX in the middle of the night. We took our way to the house, taking care to keep in the shadows of the trees. When we got to the porch the professor opened his bag and took out a silver crucifix, garlic blossoms, and a sacred wafer.

"We must guard ourselves from our enemy," he said.

Dr. Seward pulled the rusty bolt on the door until it shot back with a clang. Once inside, we all lit our lamps. The place was

thick with dust and in the corners were masses of spiders' webs.

"Which is the way to the chapel?" asked the professor.

A map of the house was included in the legal papers I had found, so I had an idea of its direction. I led the way down a passage and found the low, arched door of the chapel. We were prepared for some unpleasantness as we opened the door, but none of us expected the place to smell so foul. It was as if the monster's breath was clinging to the air. Although the stench was almost unbearable, we had to continue our search.

We found some of the earth boxes, but there were only twenty-nine left out of fifty! The professor wrenched the top off one of them. He took a piece of the sacred wafer and laid it on the earth inside. We helped him to sterilize the other boxes in the same way. Then I saw Arthur step back suddenly, and I noticed a mass of little eyes, which twinkled like stars. The whole place was alive with rats. They seemed to swarm over the place, the lamplight shining on their moving dark bodies and glittering eyes. We all hurried to the door and closed it behind us. As we left the house, the shadow of dread seemed to slip from us like a robe.

The sacred wafer

Wine is served in a silver chalice.

Sacred offerings

The sacred wafer (flat, unleavened bread) is used in Holy Communion, in which bread and wine (standing for the body and blood of Christ) is offered.

Crucifix

The professor's crucifix was a particularly powerful weapon against vampires because it was made of silver – a pure metal that was believed to deter vampires.

Chapter eight

DR. SEWARD'S DIARY

October 2

I T WAS STILL DARK when we returned home. We went upstairs to make
sure that Mina was safe. Van Helsing turned the handle of her bedroom
door, but it would not open. We threw ourselves against it, and with a
crash we burst into the room. In the moonlight we saw Mina kneeling on the
bed. By her side stood a tall, thin man clad in black. The instant we saw him
we all recognized the count. With his left hand he held back both Mina's
hands, his right hand gripped her by the back of the neck. Her white
nightdress was smeared with blood.

The count turned his face, and the hellish look that I had heard described
seemed to leap into it. His eyes flamed red with devilish passion; and the
white sharp teeth, behind the full lips of the blood-dripping mouth,
champed together like those of a wild beast. With a wrench, which threw
his victim back upon the bed as though hurled from a height, he turned and
sprang at us. But the professor was ready and held toward him the sacred
wafer. The count cowered back. Further and further he cowered, as we, lifting
our crucifixes, advanced. The moonlight suddenly failed, as a black cloud sailed
across the sky; and, when the gaslight sprang up under Quincey's match, we saw
nothing but a faint mist which trailed under the door.

Mina held her hands in front of her face and shuddered while Jonathan tried
to comfort her.

"Do not fear, my dear," said the professor. "You are quite safe here with us to
guard you. Let me hold this sacred wafer on your forehead to cleanse you. "

There was a fearful scream. The wafer had burned a mark on Mina's
forehead. "I am unclean! Even God the Almighty shuns my
polluted flesh!" she sobbed. Jonathan held her tight. Then
we all kneeled down together and swore to rescue
Mina from this terrible curse.

His eyes flamed red with
devilish passion.

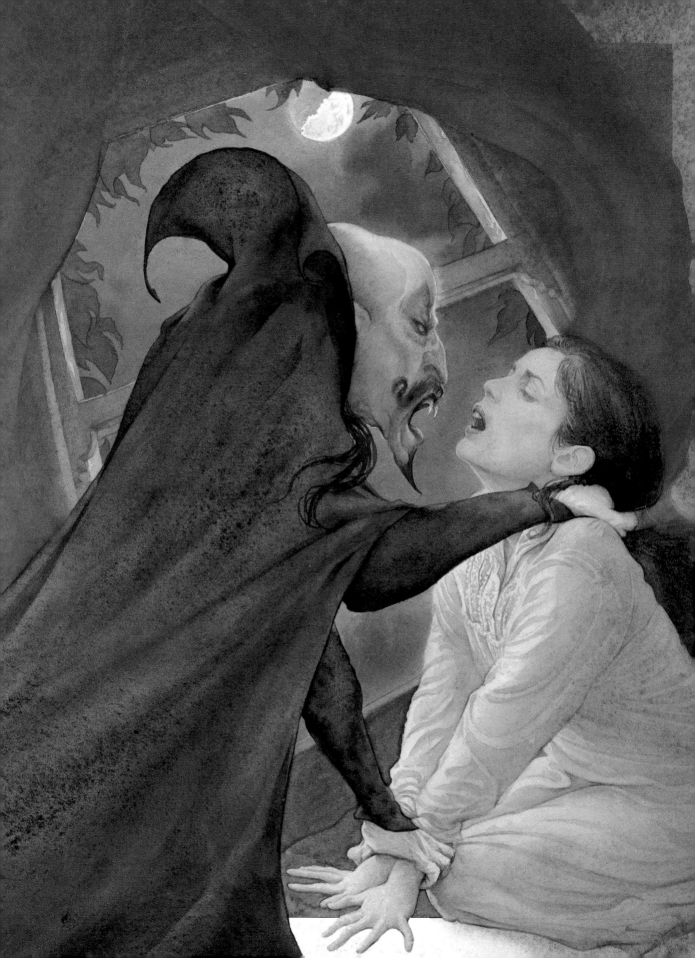

October 3

Van Helsing suggested that we would find the remaining boxes in Dracula's house in Piccadilly, which Jonathan had discovered had been bought by the count under an assumed name.

Mina agreed to stay behind, and we knew she would be safe until sunset. We took a cab to the house. We found the windows were encrusted with dust, and the shutters were up. Arthur had brought a bunch of skeleton keys; after trying several in the lock, he found one that opened the front door. Once again, the smell inside the house was terrible. We went to explore, not knowing whether the count was in the house or not.

In the dining room we found most of the earth boxes, but one was still missing. We did not lose any time in opening the boxes and treating them with the professor's holy wafer. Then we started to examine the other objects in the room: a bundle of papers, a clothes brush, a jug and basin, and a heap of keys. Suddenly, with a single bound, the count leaped into the room. When he saw us, a horrible snarl passed over his face, showing his long, pointed teeth. Jonathan advanced with a kukri knife in his hand. He lunged forward but the count leaped back in time to save himself. The knife just cut his coat and a stream of gold coins fell out. I moved forward holding a crucifix in my left hand, a knife in my right. For a moment, the count cowered back, but the next instant he dashed across the room and threw himself at the window. Amid a crash of falling glass, he tumbled onto the ground below. We saw him spring to his feet. Then he turned and spoke to us:

"You think you have left me without a place to rest; but I have more. My revenge is just begun!" With a sneer, he disappeared across the yard and through the stable door.

There was not time to pursue him, for we had to return to Mina before sunset.

Suddenly, with a single bound, the Count leaped into the room.

Skeleton keys
These are keys designed to fit many locks. They were usually used by the police – or by burglars.

Kukri knife
The large, curved blade of the kukri knife makes it a deadly fighting weapon. It was used by the Gurkhas of Nepal, a people renowned for their bravery.

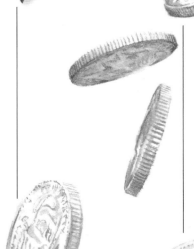

→ Overland route

→ Dracula's route

THE JOURNEY
The vampire-hunters traveled on the Orient Express to Varna, in Bulgaria. Dracula's ship followed a regular trading route to the south of Europe.

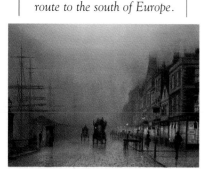

Wharf
The Thames River was lined with many boatyards (wharfs) named after their owners or the type of goods they dealt with.

Ship
The Czarina Catherine would have looked like this merchant ship, which could travel long distances.

Chapter nine

JONATHAN HARKER'S DIARY

October 4

MINA WAS WAITING FOR US when we returned. Thank God she was quite safe. We had supper together, which cheered us all up somewhat, and we told Mina everything. When we came to the part where I had rushed at the count, the professor exclaimed: "I believe the count meant to escape! He saw that with one earth box left, and a pack of men following like dogs after a fox, London was no place for him. He has taken the last earth box and has gone back to his castle in Transylvania."

Then the professor added: "He will have to travel by ship, which will take at least three weeks. We can travel overland by train to the same place in three days."

Now we must discover on what boat Count Dracula made his escape.

She sailed from Doolittle's Wharf for Varna.

October 5

Professor Van Helsing and I made enquiries at the Port of London. There we found that only one ship departed for the Black Sea

54

yesterday. She is called the *Czarina Catherine*, and she sailed from Doolittle's Wharf for Varna.

So off we went to the wharf, and there we found a fellow in a small, wooden office. When we asked him about the *Czarina Catherine*, he told us that a tall, pale man dressed all in black had brought a great box on board the ship just before she sailed on the ebb tide. At least we know that the count cannot cross running water, so he cannot leave the ship. Our best hope is to meet the *Czarina Catherine* in Varna between sunrise and sunset; for then the count will still be in his box, and cannot struggle.

October 15, Varna

We left Charing Cross Station on the morning of the 12th, arriving in Paris the same night, and there we boarded the Orient Express. We traveled night and day, arriving here in Varna at about five o'clock. Mina sleeps a great deal; throughout the journey she slept nearly all the time. Just before sunset and sunrise, however, she was very wakeful and alert.

The count cannot leave the ship, and to avoid suspicion must remain in the box. If we go on board after sunrise, he will be at our mercy.

We can only wait until the count reaches the Dardanelles and crosses the Black Sea to arrive here in Varna.

Orient Express
This luxurious train ran from Paris, across Europe to Varna, and then on to Constantinople, now Istanbul, in Turkey.

Black Sea
Dracula's ship crossed the Black Sea. This is an inland sea between southeastern Europe and Asia.

Ports
The ports of the Black Sea were used for fishing, trade, and transport. They were well connected by rivers to towns farther inland.

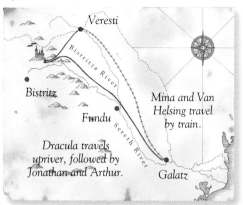

Morris & Seward's route

The chase
Morris and Seward followed Dracula by riding on horseback along the bank of the Bistritza River. They rode up to the Borgo Pass and met up with Jonathan and Arthur there.

Telegram
A telegram was the quickest way of communicating over long distances. A message could reach its destination in a day.

Chapter ten

Mina Harker's diary

October 28

I T IS MOST STRANGE. There is no news of the ship and she ought to be here by now. We were all concerned, so Arthur contacted the Port of London by telegram. He received a telegram by return:

OCTOBER 28 – TELEGRAM, LONDON, TO ARTHUR HOLMWOOD, VARNA
CZARINA CATHERINE REPORTED ENTERING GALATZ AT ONE O'CLOCK TODAY.

The count has tricked us! We must leave for Galatz as soon as possible. Fortunately I have learned the train times by heart. The next train departs at 6:30 tomorrow morning.

November 6

We traveled through Bucharest and on to Galatz in an agony of expectation. On arrival, Arthur took me to the hotel while Jonathan and the two doctors went directly to the port. They returned with heavy hearts. The captain of the *Czarina Catherine* reported that the earth box had been removed from the ship before sunrise by some gypsies.

Everyone is tired and dispirited. But while the men rested, I studied the maps, and I do believe I have made a discovery. When everyone was gathered together once more, I explained that Count Dracula must be returning to his own place by water, as this is the most safe and secret way. We know that the count is using gypsies to take him home and, according to the maps, the Sereth River is the most suitable route. It is, at Fundu, joined by the Bistritza, which runs close to Dracula's castle.

The others were delighted with my conclusion.

"I will take care of Mina," said the professor.

I could see that Jonathan wanted to be with me, but he was determined to destroy the ... the vampire.

Dr. Seward and Quincey Morris departed on horseback, Jonathan and Arthur followed up the river in a steamboat, while the professor and I took the train to Veresti. From there we traveled toward the Borgo Pass. The country got wilder and the snow began to fall as we neared the mountains.

It was late in the afternoon when we saw where the clear line of Dracula's castle cut the sky. Professor Van Helsing searched around in the snow for a sheltered spot. He found a hollow in which we could wait for the others.

We saw where the clear line of Dracula's castle cut the sky.

Suddenly he called out: "Look, Mina!" I looked through his binoculars and saw, in the distance, a group of gypsies on horseback coming from the river, pulling a cart. On the cart was a great box. Looking round, I saw three more horsemen following at breakneck speed. "They are racing for the sunset," cried the professor.

Closer and closer they drew. Then I heard Jonathan shout, "Halt!" The gypsies slowed down and surrounded the cart. Their knives flashed, but Arthur and Dr. Seward held them at gunpoint. In an instant Jonathan had jumped up on the cart and prized the lid off the box with his knife. The group had drawn very close to the place where we were sheltering, and I could see the count lying within the box upon the earth, deathly pale. As I watched, his eyes saw the sinking sun, and the look of hate in them turned to triumph. But at that moment came the flash of Jonathan's great knife.

I shrieked as I saw it shear through the throat; while at the same moment Mr. Morris plunged his bowie knife into the heart. The whole body crumbled to dust before our eyes.

The castle of Dracula now stood out against the red sky, and every stone of its broken battlements was shown up against the light of the setting sun.

The gypsies turned and rode away, frightened for their lives. I flew to Jonathan's side. The sun was now right down upon the mountaintop, and the red light fell upon my face. Everyone turned toward me and, with one impulse, they sank to their knees. Then Jonathan smiled at me and said: "God be thanked that all has not been in vain. Your forehead is as white as the snow again! The curse has passed away."

The whole body crumbled to dust.

THE BOOK AND THE LEGEND

Beliefs vary, but generally a vampire is a dead human who returns from the grave and sucks the blood of the living. Vampire myths are rooted in the idea of blood as the source of life, and that drinking it would renew strength. Bram Stoker got many of his ideas about vampires by reading about the legends of eastern Europe. But he also added some of his own ideas and brought the vampire legend up to date.

What do vampires look like?

Many vampires from eastern European folklore had a deathly pale complexion like that of a corpse, and had a strong smell of death. Transylvanian vampires had foul breath and were horribly ugly, with hypnotic blood-red eyes. In the novel, Dracula has pale skin and long fingernails. His eyes flashed red when he was angry. His very red lips covered long, pointed teeth.

No soul

The idea that vampires had no reflection was first introduced in Dracula. This was based on a religious belief that a mirror reflects a person's soul (Dracula had no soul, so no reflection appeared). Today, some people still believe that breaking a mirror brings bad luck – if you damage a mirror, you harm your soul.

Dracula's age varies. When Jonathan sees him again in London he has "grown young," probably because he has recently feasted on the life-giving blood of Lucy.

Dracula turns himself into a wolf when he enters Lucy's bedroom.

In folklore, bats were often linked to the devil, and believed to be a sign of death.

Transformation

A vampire's ability to change shape is common throughout folklore and was often linked to witchcraft. Dracula becomes a bat and listens to the vampire-hunters' plans to catch him, and he turns into a mist when he leaves Mina's bedroom. In Romania, vampires were believed to appear as points of light in the air – like dust.

DESTROYING VAMPIRES

In folklore, there were many ways of destroying a vampire. Some of the methods included shooting it with a silver bullet, exposing it to sunlight, chopping off its head, and burning the creature's body.

Hammer and stake

The most common method was to hammer a wooden stake through the vampire's heart. It was a means of fixing the body to the ground.

Bowie knife

In the novel, Stoker has the vampires killed in traditional as well as new ways. Lucy is destroyed by the stake, while Dracula himself is killed by a bowie knife; a modern weapon in Stoker's time.

Protection against vampires

Strong-smelling garlic was used to detect and to ward off vampires. Another method was to scatter seeds on the vampire's coffin – which was believed to keep it inside. Hawthorn was hung over doorways or grown around houses.

Garlic

Hawthorn

Christianity

Christianity as a force of good was a natural enemy of vampires. Any Christian symbol could be used as a weapon against a vampire. The main religion in Romania was the Orthodox Church, which had many connections with the Catholic Church.

Sacred wafer

Crucifix

Candlelight

Candles were used to ward off all kinds of evil. The light of a candle traditionally represents sunlight or the light of Christ, hence its use in Christian ceremonies. In Romania the candle was one of the main protections against vampires.

THE HISTORY OF VAMPIRES

Vampire stories can be traced back to ancient civilizations. The earliest known picture of a bloodsucking human appears on a Babylonian cylinder seal, from about 4,000 years ago. In India, tales were written about a vampire who hangs upside down in a tree, like a bat. Vampires also appear in the legends of ancient Egypt, China, Rome, and Greece.

Striges, a vampire-witch from ancient Greece

Vampires in eastern Europe

In the 16th and 17th centuries, vampire legends developed throughout eastern Europe. In Hungary, a countess called Elizabeth Bathory was accused of torturing and murdering young women. It was said she bit her victims' flesh and drank their blood.

The sinister castle of Csejthe, where Bathory lived, today lies in ruins.

Ellizabeth Bathory (1560–1614)

Transylvania

Vampire folklore flourished in the remote mountainous land of Transylvania, with its rich mix of ethnic groups and traditions. Here people believed that you would become a vampire if you were born with teeth, or if you were the seventh son of a seventh son.

In eastern Europe, many people thought that epidemics, like the bubonic plague, were caused by the devil and that the victims became vampires.

Transylvanian people believed that if a cat jumped over a body before it was buried, the dead person might become a vampire.

Vampire literature

Vampire tales spread across Europe in the late 1700s and vampires soon began to appear in literature. Before *Dracula*, the most influential book was *The Vampyre* (1819), a short story published by John Polidori, based on a tale by Lord Byron. Another early vampire story was *Varney the Vampire* (1847).

After Dracula

A lthough Bram Stoker wrote several novels, he is remembered for just one. *Dracula* still frightens and fascinates readers, one hundred years after it first appeared in 1897. However, it is the movies based on the book, not the book itself, that have turned Dracula into the popular mythical figure he is today.

Peter Cushing became famous for his portrayal of the intellectual vampire-hunter Van Helsing.

BRAM STOKER

Bram (Abraham) Stoker (1847–1912) was born in Dublin, Ireland. After studying mathematics at Trinity College, Dublin, he worked as a civil servant. Stoker was fascinated with vampire literature, and in his spare time began to write his own horror stories.

Bram Stoker

Lee and Cushing

In 1958, the British actors Christopher Lee and Peter Cushing teamed up to play Dracula and Van Helsing in the movie *Horror of Dracula*. It was the first movie of the book in full color, which it used to great effect.

Lee created a new image for Dracula that was closer to the original novel. He had fangs, which he sank into his female victims' throats. Lee went on to make many Dracula movies.

Henry Irving

Stoker's other main interest was the theater. He became close friends with the actor Henry Irving, and was appointed his stage manager in London. Here, Stoker began to do research into Transylvania and its vampire traditions, and the idea for *Dracula* took shape.

Stoker may have based Dracula on the forceful figure of Henry Irving.

Early British edition

French edition, 1920

Hungarian actor, Bela Lugosi

Nosferatu

Max Shreck was the first actor to portray Dracula on screen in the German silent movie *Nosferatu*. Because permission to make a movie version of the novel had not been given, the title and the characters' names were changed.

First editions

Dracula was published in May, 1897. It met with widespread success and was soon translated into many languages.

On stage

In 1924, *Dracula* was presented on stage in England. The play was a great success and moved to Broadway. Here, Bela Lugosi, wearing formal black evening attire and a cape, played the title role. He later appeared in the first talking movie based on the novel, and his portrayal was soon copied worldwide.

VAMPIRE MOVIES

Below are some of the major films inspired by Dracula and the vampire theme:

DATE	MOVIE / STAR
1922	Nosferatu, *starring Max Shreck*
1931	Dracula, *starring Bela Lugosi*
1958	Horror of Dracula, *starring Christopher Lee*
1979	Love at First Bite, *starring George Hamilton*
1979	Dracula, *starring Frank Langella*
1979	Nosferatu: the Vampyre, *starring Klaus Kinski*
1992	Bram Stoker's Dracula, *starring Gary Oldman*
1994	Interview with the Vampire, *starring Tom Cruise*

Cartoon count
Dracula has also inspired a whole range of books, comics, and cartoon characters, such as Count Duckula, a popular cartoon character of the 1980s. Count Duckula lived in Castle Duckula in Transylvania, and slept in a magic coffin that could take him and his castle around the world.

Brides of Dracula, France, 1966

International Dracula
Movie versions of *Dracula* appeared throughout Europe, as well as in North America and Britain.

Italian film poster for the German/French film Nosferatu: the Vampyre

KLAUS KINSKI   ISABELLE ADJANI

Nosferatu
IL PRINCIPE DELLA NOTTE

con BRUNO GANZ

sceneg. prodotto e diretto da WERNER HERZOG

LA SANGRE DEL VAMPIRO
EASTMANCOLOR

DONALD WOLFIT · BARBARA SHELLEY

Blood of the Vampire, Spain, 1966

DRACULA LIVES ON
The myth of Dracula has boosted the tourist industry in Tranyslvania. Places to see include Bran Castle and the Borgo Pass, where a new Dracula Castle Hotel has been built.

Shreck's frightening portrayal of Dracula

The true Dracula?
The movie that is closest to the original story is *Bram Stoker's Dracula*, with Gary Oldman as the count. It includes references to Vlad Dracula.

Vampire societies
Some people still believe that vampires exist. There is a Vampire Research Center in New York that investigates reports of active vampires from all over the world. The mystery of the vampire lives on . . .

Acknowledgments

Picture Credits

The publisher would like to thank the following for their kind permission to reproduce their photographs:

t=top, b=bottom, a=above,
c=center, l=left, r=right.

AKG Photo London: 8tc; Erich Lessing back jacket cla.
Ancient Art and Architecture: Ronald Sheridan 61cr.
Elizabeth Bacon: 27cr, 63br.
Gerard Boullay: 61bc.
Bridgeman Art Library, London: Christopher Wood Gallery, London 54cl; Forbes Magazine Collection, New York 33cr; Kunsthistorisches Museum, Vienna 18tl; Phillips the Auctioneers 11cr; Roy Miles Gallery, London 32tl.
British Museum, London: 17tr, 20bl, 61tr.
Jean-Loup C harmet, Paris: 8bra, 8bl, 23tr, 61ca, 61cra, 61cb, 62bla.
ET Archive: 20cl.
Mary Evans Picture Library: 18bl, 30cl, 48bl, 55br, 61br, 62cl, back jacket flap tl.
Fortean Picture Library: Derek Stafford 60tl.
Chris Fraser: 41tr.
Glasgow Museums: front jacket c.
Ronald Grant Archive: Hammer Films 62c; 42bl, 62/63 full page.

Kurt Hielscher: 12bl.
Michael Holford: 44tl.
Hulton Getty Picture Collection: 38tl, 62clb.
Hutchison Library: J. Henderson 8c.
Images Colour Library: 13tr, 46bl.
Impact: Jon Hoffman 14bl, Robert Gibbs 14tl.
Kobal Collection: 33tr, 62bc, 62br, 63bc.
Simon Marsden: 7 full page.
NHPA: John Shaw 13cr.
National Maritime Museum, London: 28tl, 29tr, 29cr, 54bl.
National Trust Photographic Library: Andreas von Einsiedel 35tr.
Planet Earth Pictures: John Lythgoe 55cr.
Rosenbach Museum and Library, New York: 62clb.
Spectrum Colour Library: 55tr.
Tony Stone Images: Ken Biggs 30tl; Richard Kaylin 44cl.
Viewfinder: 12cl.
Vintage Magazine Company: 38cl, 62tr, 63tc, 63tcr, 63cra.
Jerry Young: 44clb, 60bl.

Additional photography: Andy Crawford and Gary Ombler at the DK Photographic Studio; Richard Leaney; Alex Wilson; Victoria Hall.

Additional illustrations: Sallie Alane Reason; Stephen Raw.

DK would particularly like to thank the following people:

Jo Bacon; Bridgeman Art Library; Jo Carlill; ET Archive; Mary Evans Picture Library; Leah Gordon and Annabel Edwards, for permission to photograph the metal-work sculpture on p.21, (br), artist: Gabriel Bien-Aimée, original work entitled *Dancing with the Birds of the Night* ; Victoria Hall for research assistance; Joanna Hartley; The Post Office Archives, London; Risky Business, London; Themis at the Werner Forman Archive; Alexandra Warwick for her advice and loan of costumes and accessories; Marion Dent for proofreading; the following people and institutions in Transylvania: Raoul Mihail, Bianca, and all at Bran Castle; Gabriela Chiru and Juana at the Ethnographical Museum, Brasov; everyone at the Transylvanian Museum of Ethnography, Cluj-Napoca; the History Museum of Transylvania, Cluj-Napoca; George Szirtes.